A Fistful of Pearls

and other tales from Iraq

Retold by Elizabeth

Illustrated by Shelle

F

FRANCES LINCOLN
CHILDREN'S BOOKS

Contents

Introduction

I lived in Iraq for a while, years ago. In those days, many parts of the country were much as they had been for centuries. You could still visit friends in the cool, roomy old houses along the banks of the Tigris, where pet gazelles nibbled grass in the courtyards. The old souks were still there: narrow roofed lanes lined with little brightly lit shops, where merchants sat cross-legged on carpeted platforms, offering their customers tiny cups of coffee. In corners of old cities like Baghdad, Mosul and Basra there were narrow alleys free of cars, and you could look up at the carved lattice-work of window shutters and step through archways into shady courtyards. It was in one of these that I was once told stories of a cannibal mother and a stone-throwing jinn.

Above the houses rose the domes and minarets of ancient mosques, and from them sang out, five times a day, the beautiful Muslim call to prayer.

Much of Iraq is desert. You can drive for miles and see only a few villages built of mud bricks, little shepherd boys minding flocks of sheep and goats and, from time to time, the long, low black tents of the Bedouin nomads. Sometimes, in the heat, mirages appear on the horizon.

"Look! A lake! A palace! A forest of trees!" you shout. But the wonders disappear as you approach, and all that's there are clumps of dry thorn bushes among a scatter of stones.

In the north of Iraq are cooler green hills and beyond them a range of high spiky mountains. The Kurdish people live here. Their villages climb the hillsides on terraces of stone, shaded by fig and mulberry trees. In the spring, wild tulips and hollyhocks sprout everywhere, and the air is full of birdsong.

The south of Iraq is quite different. When I lived there, a great marsh stretched for many miles. Giant reeds, taller than people, swayed in the wind above the shallow water. The Marsh Arabs had lived in the same way in this watery world for thousands of years. They had created little islands and on them they built wonderful houses woven from the reeds. They caught fat fish in the water and kept buffaloes and chickens. When you paddled from island to island along the waterways in a canoe, you couldn't see any distance ahead because of the reeds towering over you. It was like being an ant walking through a lawn.

Great changes were coming to Iraq even when I lived there. The modern world was sweeping away the old houses by the Tigris to make room for motorways. People were watching TV instead of telling the old stories to each other. Lorries, rather than caravans of camels, were carrying goods from city to city.

Tyranny brought terrible suffering to the people of Iraq. Hundreds of thousands died in a brutal war against Iran. Villages were bombed, a large part of the marshes was drained and secret policemen spied on the people. But times became even harder when foreign powers invaded the country. Bombs ripped through crowded market places. Beautiful mosques were blown up and fear came to everyone as the country was ripped apart.

I haven't been back to Iraq, but in spite of all that has happened there, I know that many lovely things remain. I'm sure that wild pelicans still swoop over the great twin rivers Tigris and Euphrates, and children dive in and jump out of the water like happy frogs. The roller birds must still flutter from tree to tree, showing off their brilliant turquoise wings. Mirages in the desert will always deceive the traveller. The waters are creeping back to the drained marshes, bringing the reeds, the fish and the birds with them.

Like everywhere else in the world, there are still misers and boastful people and lazy ones and those with fiery tempers who need to be taught a lesson, and there are still kind, hospitable neighbours and shrewd men and women and beautiful girls and handsome men, just as there were in the great days of the Caliph a thousand years ago, when the stories in this book were already being told. Children in Iraq still love to hear the stories of clever Firuz the hare, Zirak the rat, and the wolf who made sheepskin coats.

I hope you'll enjoy them too.

Elizabeth Laird

Who knows when these stories happened,
Or at what time of the day?
Perhaps they never happened at all!
There is no truth except in God.

Typical saying used to introduce a story in Iraq

Lazy Ahmed

In the old days, when time stood on its head and who knows what was what, there was a lazy man called Ahmed. He never did a stroke of work, and if any one asked him to lend a hand, he'd say, "My poor back. It hurts too much for that kind of thing," or, "I can't do anything just now. It's nearly dinner-time." Then he'd roll over and go back to sleep.

Ahmed's wife was called Jarada, which means 'Locust'. She, poor woman, was at her wit's end. Her husband brought no money home, and she had to scrape around every day to find enough to eat.

"Husband," she told Ahmed, "you must go out and earn some money. There isn't a single dinar in the house."

"Not today," Ahmed said, yawning. "I don't feel like it. Who'd give me a job, anyway?"

But one day clever Jarada had an idea.

"You don't need to find a job," she said. "Just put on a big turban, so that you'll look like a wise man, and find a shady corner in the market place. Sit down there, and tell everyone who passes that you're a magician. Say that you can read secrets and write charms."

Ahmed cheered up at the thought of sitting in a shady corner in the market place. Then his eyes opened wide with alarm.

"But I can't read people's secrets!" he objected. "And I can't write charms. I can't read or write at all, as well you know."

"Don't be so feeble," said Jarada. "Charms are not meant to be read. Just scribble on a piece of paper and tell your customer it's written in a special magic language."

"Well, I suppose I could do that," said Ahmed, "but not till after lunch."

"There will be no lunch," his wife said firmly, "until you earn some money to buy it."

She wound a huge turban round his head, tucked a pen case into his belt and put some paper in his hand, and off went Ahmed to the market place.

Although Ahmed was so lazy, he was a kind man and he enjoyed listening to people's troubles and making sympathetic noises. Wives asked him for charms to make their husbands love them.

Soldiers asked for magic amulets to keep them safe in war, and parents asked for spells to protect their babies. Everyone went away feeling happier after they'd talked to Ahmed. They took with them his scribbled bits of paper, and he knotted the coins they gave him into the end of his sash.

Soon Ahmed had more money than he'd ever earned in his life, and his fame spread through the city.

One day, an anxious-looking girl sat down in front of him.

"Please sir, you must help me," she whispered.

"Of course I will, my dear," said Ahmed, nodding his turbaned head.

"And you promise to keep my secret?" the girl went on.

"My lips are sealed," said Ahmed.

"Well then," the girl said, her voice trembling, "I'm a servant at the Caliph's palace, and I've done a terrible thing." She leaned closer, and whispered in Ahmed's ear, "I was cleaning the Caliph's room, and I saw his jewelled ring lying there. 'Take it!' whispered Satan in my ear. I was tempted, and I took it! Now there's a great fuss going on at the palace, and I'm scared they'll catch me. I wish I'd never taken it. I'm not a real thief! You're a magician. Tell me, will I be caught? And if I am, what will they do to me?"

Ahmed shook his head gravely.

"You must give the ring back," he said, "or lose your head."

"But how can I do it without being found out?"

Ahmed thought for a moment.

"Hide the ring in a lump of dough, and feed it to one of the ducks that swim about on the pool in the palace garden. Be sure to mark the beak of the same duck with a dab of henna dye. You'll be safe, if you do what I say."

The girl hurried off, and Ahmed went home to tell Jarada what he'd done.

"Very good, husband," she said. "Now, leave the next part to me."

The next day, Jarada put on her veil, and hurried to the palace. The ring had still not been found, and there was a great fuss and bother as everyone hunted for it.

"The Caliph should send for Ahmed," she told one of the women servants. "He's a wonderful magician. He'd find the ring in no time."

The woman servant told the Caliph's gardener, and the Caliph's gardener told the Caliph's groom, and the Caliph's groom told the Caliph's cook, and the Caliph's cook whispered a word in the ear of the Caliph's Grand Vizier, and that very same afternoon the Caliph sent for Ahmed.

"I hear you're a great magician," he said, looking doubtfully at the roly-poly figure of Ahmed, topped by his enormous turban.

Ahmed bowed very low.

"I am, peace be upon Your Excellency," he said, "and if you will do me the honour of showing me your garden, your ring will be back on your finger again by tonight."

The Caliph escorted Ahmed to his garden, and there, paddling serenely across the pool, was a plump little duck with a dab of henna dye on her beak.

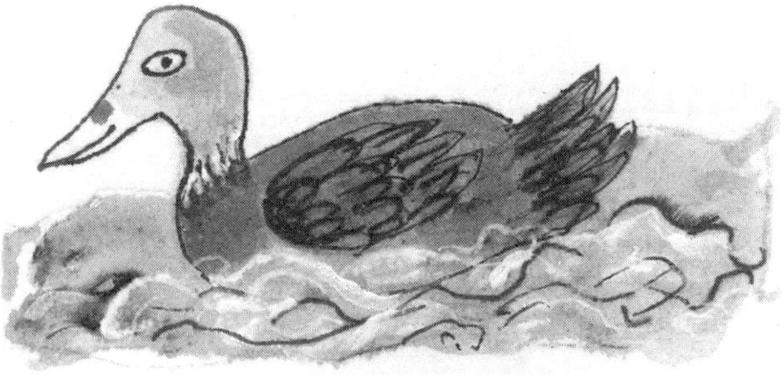

"If you kill that duck, and stuff her with nuts and spices and serve her to me on a bed of saffron rice," said greedy Ahmed, "I promise that your ring will be returned to you."

Of course, as soon as the Caliph's cook opened up the duck, out fell the ring, winking and sparkling in the light of day. So that night, Ahmed feasted with the Caliph on the best meal of his life, and went home with a purse of gold in his pocket.

Ahmed was famous now. People came from far and wide to consult him. He and his wife lived happily and he grew fatter than ever.

But one day, a gang of forty robbers broke into the palace and stole a chest full of jewels and money. The Caliph sent for Ahmed at once.

"Find my chest!" he commanded. "It will be an easy matter for a magician like you."

Ahmed went pale and shook in his shoes.

"I don't think...... that is to say...... I'm not sure......" he began.

The Caliph's eyes flashed fire.

"Are you a magician or a fraud?" he demanded. "If you don't restore my chest to me, I'll have your head instead."

"But I need time!" wailed Ahmed. "A delicate matter, such as this..."

"How long?" asked the Caliph.

"Forty days," said Ahmed, not daring to ask for longer.

"Very well," said the Caliph. "You have forty days. I'll have my treasure, or I'll have your head."

"I hear and obey," said Ahmed, bowing low, and he scurried out of the palace and ran home in great distress.

"See what your cleverness has led to!" he said to Jarada. "This is all your fault. Now all I can do is pray."

News spread around the city that the Caliph had sent for the great magician Ahmed, who would certainly find the treasure chest. It even reached the ears of the robbers themselves.

"If this magician is as great as people say, then we are in danger," the robber chief said to his thirty-nine companions. "We must find out how much he knows." So he sent one of his men to listen at the window of Ahmed's house.

Ahmed was lying on his bed, tossing and turning in misery. He had only forty days to solve this great mystery, and the first day was nearly over already.

"Oh Jarada, my little Locust, one of the forty is passing!" he moaned to his wife.

The robber listening at the window jumped back in amazement, and ran back to the robber band.

"Chief, that man is an amazing magician," he panted. "While I listened at his window, I heard him say to his wife, 'One of the forty is passing.'"

"Hmm, worrying news," said the robber chief, stroking his long moustache. "We must find out more. Another one of you must go and listen at this man's window tomorrow."

So the next night, another robber laid his ear to the crack in Ahmed's window, just as Ahmed groaned to his wife, "Oh my darling little Locust, one of the forty has gone, and now another is passing!"

The robber ran away so fast that his robe flew out behind him. When he heard what the second man had to say, the robber chief went pale and tugged at his moustache.

"If he knows everything, we're done for!" he exclaimed, "but you might not have heard him properly. Another man must go tonight."

The third robber was listening at the crack of Ahmed's window, when Ahmed, pacing up and down, cried out, "Oh my poor little Locust! Just think! Another of the forty is passing!"

The third robber's knees knocked so hard he could hardly run, but somehow or other he staggered back to his chief.

"The man's a devil!" spluttered the robber chief, and he pulled so hard at his long black beard that a tuft came away in his hand. "There's no help for it. We must go to this great magician and throw ourselves on his mercy, before he goes to the Caliph and tells him everything."

Ahmed was tossing and turning in an uneasy sleep when the robbers knocked on his door. He started up in terror, and his eyes rolled with fright in his moon-round face when he saw the forty robbers standing on his doorstep. They filed into

his house and stood politely, all squashed up together, trying not to knock over the furniture.

When Ahmed heard the chief's stammering story, he couldn't believe his luck, but he frowned and tried to looked very stern.

"You are all wicked men," he said, with great dignity, "and deserve whatever punishment the Caliph chooses. However, I'm a merciful man and I won't betray you. But there's one condition. You must tell me where the treasure's hidden, so that I can return it to its rightful owner."

The robber chief threw himself down in front of Ahmed with tears of gratitude in his eyes.

"To save our lives, we'd sacrifice more than a chest full of treasure!" he said. "We'll tell you where it's hidden, and we'll give you bags of gold, and what's more, we'll promise never, ever to come and rob your house."

The youngest robber had furtively picked up one of Jarada's best spoons, but he quickly put it down again. Then the chief told Ahmed where the treasure was hidden, and they all filed out.

The next morning, Ahmed hurried to the palace.

"Your Sublimity," he said the Caliph, "your treasure chest is found! Come with me and I'll show you where it's hidden."

So the Caliph and his vizier and his grooms and a few of his soldiers went out into the desert and Ahmed showed them the very bush behind which the treasure was hidden. When they opened it up and counted it all, not one piece was missing.

The Caliph was delighted, and gave Ahmed a magnificent new house and servants, and even more bags of gold than the robber chief had given him.

From then on, the Caliph boasted about his wonderful magician to everyone. People came from far and wide to see the famous man.

"Oh my little Locust," sighed Ahmed. "This is all too much. It's such an effort seeing all these people, and besides, one day I'm sure to be found out. What shall we do then?"

At that very moment, the Caliph's servant knocked on the door.

"You're to come to the palace at once, your honour," he said with a low bow. "The Caliph wants to show you off to a prince who's visiting from a foreign country."

Ahmed began to tremble.

"You see?" he said to Jarada. "What did I say? Pray for me, my little Locust. There's no help for me now but Allah."

At the palace, the Caliph smiled at the sight of Ahmed's round little figure approaching.

"Here he comes!" he said to the foreign prince. "Here's my amazing magician. This man can see inside the bellies of ducks, and knows what's buried beneath the earth. Just watch this." He held out one closed fist to Ahmed. "Tell me, magician, what I'm holding in my hand."

Everything seemed to go black in front of Ahmed's eyes and he groaned aloud in terror.

"Ah, Locust! Locust!" he cried out. "Caught at last!"

“There!” said the Caliph delightedly. “What did I tell you?” He opened his fist and out flew a locust.

“Test him again,” said the foreign prince. “What else can he do?”

But Ahmed, quite overcome with fright, had fallen down at the Caliph’s feet in a dead faint.

Now clever Jarada, afraid of what might happen, had sent a servant to follow her husband, and had given him careful instructions. The servant now rushed in and began to weep and wail.

“Oh my master! My poor master!” he wailed. “The strain of all this has killed him!”

Ahmed opened one eye, and quickly shut it again.

“How terrible,” said the Caliph sadly. “I had no idea that magic was such hard work. Take the poor man away and bury him.”

Ahmed, keeping absolutely still, was carried all the way home, but as soon as he was safe inside his house, he jumped up and embraced Jarada.

“My clever Locust, I’m sure it was you who saved me,” he said. “But there’s going to be no more magic again. Ever.”

“There’ll be no need,” said his wife. “We have enough money to last us for the rest of our lives.

We'll tell the Caliph that you have miraculously recovered, but that your magical powers have deserted you."

News of Ahmed's recovery, and the loss of his powers, spread through Baghdad. The Caliph was so happy to hear that his favourite magician had not died after all, that he showered him with yet more riches.

Ahmed and Jarada lived in comfort and happiness all their days, and Ahmed never had to do another stroke of work again.

Zirak and the Ring-Dove

Once there was a bird-catcher who used to lay his net out on the ground and scatter seed on it to attract the birds. Down they would fly, cheeping with joy at the sight of the seeds, but once they had started pecking – *snap!* – the bird-catcher would pull the strings of his net tight shut and the poor birds would all be caught.

One day, it was the turn of the Ring-Dove and her sisters to find themselves trapped in his net. They flapped about desperately trying to free themselves, but they only succeeded in tangling their feathers and claws even more firmly in the net's cruel meshes.

"Listen to me, sisters!" Ring-Dove cried. "There's only one way out of this. If we all try to save our own skins, none of us will escape. We must stay calm and work together, and then we might have a chance. Let's all try to fly, flapping our wings at the same time. We might be able to lift ourselves and the net off the ground, and fly up beyond the birdcatcher's reach."

"*Coo! Coo!* You're right! You're right!" the other doves agreed.

"Here we go, then," called out Ring-Dove. "Are you ready? Spread your wings! Push off from the ground now! Fly!"

The doves, acting together like one great bird, took off from the ground, and with a supreme effort tugged the net out of the birdcatcher's hand. He let out a shout and ran after them, jumping up into the air to try to grab hold of the net.

"Fly faster, sisters!" shouted Ring-Dove. "Fly higher, or he'll catch us!

"*Coo! Coo!* We can't! We can't!" panted the other doves.

Just then, Ring-Dove saw that they were approaching the nearby town.

"If we stay out here in the desert, he'll easily see us and pick us up when we're exhausted," she told the others. "But if we can reach the town, we'll lose him in the narrow streets. Once we get that far, I have a friend who will help us."

"*Coo! Coo!* We agree! We agree!" groaned the other doves, and a few minutes later, with a final great effort, they had flown over the outer wall of the city and were lost to the birdcatcher's view. Fuming at the loss of his net and his prey, he gave up the chase and stumped off home.

Ring-Dove guided the netful of birds to a quiet part of town. They landed, collapsing on the ground in a flutter of wings, and lay exhausted in a feathery heap.

"Now what, Ring-Dove?" they said. "You think you've been so clever, but here we all are, stuck in this net, same as before, with no way out."

"Yes, and I've bent a claw, squashed up like this," grumbled one.

"And I've lost three tail-feathers," complained another.

"It's all very well for you," scolded a third. "I'm sure my wing's broken. It feels all floppy."

Ring-Dove ignored them. She was poking her head out through the net, looking at a hole in the ground nearby.

"Zirak! It's me! Your friend Ring-Dove!" she was calling.

A rat stuck his head out of the hole.

"Ring-Dove?" he said crossly. "I don't see no Ring-Dove. Who's trying to make a fool of me? Bunch of feathers twittering like old hens, that's all I can see. I'm off back down to finish my lunch."

And he disappeared below ground again.

"Zirak!" pleaded Ring-Dove. "Come back! Have you forgotten your old friend? I need your help!"

Zirak the rat appeared again. This time he came out of his hole and cautiously approached the net.

"Well, blow me! It is you, after all," he said. "What are you doing in there, Ring-Dove, my old pal? Doesn't look like a good place to be at all."

"The birdcatcher caught us in this net," answered Ring-Dove. "We all flew up together and managed to get away from him. But we're very tired now. Chew the net for us, dear Zirak. Bite through it and get us out, before a cat comes and kills us all."

Zirak looked over his shoulder uneasily at the mention of a cat, but he twirled a gallant whisker and said nobly, "Do anything for an old chum, wouldn't I? Now let me see – this bit here first, then that bit over there, then – yes, I see how it goes. Panic not, Ring-Dove. I'll soon have you free."

But Ring-Dove shook her head.

"Not me, Zirak. Free my sisters first."

"Nah," said Zirak, his teeth champing away on the net. "*Hagetshplotherschslater.*"

"What was that?" said Ring-Dove, straining to understand.

"You first, the rest later," said Zirak, lifting up his mouth for a moment.

"If you free me first, you might get tired and leave my poor sisters to suffer," whispered Ring-Dove, who was now so exhausted, she could barely speak. "But if you leave me till last, I know you'll go on and on until we're all free."

Zirak burst out laughing.

"What a mind-reader you are, m'dear! Your sisters – silly girls, listen to 'em moaning and groaning! Can't say I'd bother to do much for them. But you – well, I'd never let you go under, not even if a cat was breathing down my neck." He shuddered at the thought, but went on cheerfully, "Right then. Here we go. Which of you grumps am I letting out first?"

"*Coo! Coo!* Me! Me! Me!" cried out all the other doves.

Zirak set to work. He chewed and he bit and he gnawed and he munched until one after the other the doves staggered out of the net and fluttered up to perch on the top of the wall above, where they smoothed their feathers and preened themselves back into a good mood, and cooed out their thanks to Zirak for rescuing them.

Ring-Dove wouldn't let Zirak tackle even one of the knots that tied her until every one of her sisters had been released. Poor Zirak's jaws were aching, and his lips were bleeding. Just as he started work on the last knot, the dreaded *miaow* of a cat could be heard not far away.

"*Coo! Coo!* Chew, Zirak, chew!" called the row of doves above.

Zirak bit through the last knot at the very moment when a lean black alley-cat came bounding into view. Ring-Dove, free at last, managed to flutter up to safety beside her sisters, just as the cat leaped up to swipe at her with

a sharp claw. Missing her, he turned to catch Zirak, only to see the rat's long pink tail disappear down his hole.

"You're a true friend, Zirak!" the Ring-Dove called out. "A true, true friend!"

"Not me, love," came Zirak's voice, echoing hollowly from the safety of his underground hole. "When it comes to friendship, you're the real thing. Putting all those silly sisters before yourself, that's true friendship. Ain't no one can hold a candle to you, girl, and that's my last word on the subject."

The Pots that had Babies

Once upon a time there was a miser. He had bags of gold and silver tucked away under his bed, but he begrudged even the crumbs the birds picked up in his garden. Hidden away in his house he had chests which were stuffed with precious jewels, but he was too stingy to put out a saucer of milk for his cat. In every room he had cupboards bursting with precious silks, but he went around in a filthy gown and a turban that was so faded, it looked like a dirty dishcloth.

If someone asked him a favour, he sent him off with a flea in his ear. If he was invited to a wedding, he refused to go, in order to save the cost of a present for the bride and groom.

Everyone was fed up with him.

"I'm going to teach that old wretch a lesson," the miser's neighbour said one day.

He went to the old man's house and knocked on the door. The miser was counting his gold coins. He jumped with surprise at the *rat-tat-tat* on the door, and knocked his piles of coins over, startling his poor, thin cat.

Now I'll have to start all over again, he thought crossly.

The neighbour knocked again.

"I'm not in!" shouted the miser. "Go away!"

The neighbour knocked a third time.

"Please," he called out, "open the door. There's something I want to ask you."

"If it's money you want, I haven't got any!" shouted the miser, sweeping all his coins out of sight. "There's no food in the house, either."

"Oh, I don't want you to give me anything," the neighbour called back.

Reluctantly, the miser opened the door a crack and peered out with one eye.

"Well?" he demanded. "What do you want?"

"Just a little, little thing," said the neighbour, smiling in the friendliest way. "My relatives are coming to my house tonight, and my wife wants to cook them a special meal. She'd like to borrow your cooking pot."

"Certainly not," the miser said, slamming the door in his face.

Ten minutes later, the neighbour's wife called with the same request, and she received the same answer. Half an hour later came the neighbour's oldest son, then his oldest daughter, then the next son and the next daughter, until at last the miser was so tired of people knocking at his door that he gave in.

"Take it, then," he said, thrusting his oldest, dirtiest pot into the arms of the smallest child of all, "but if you don't bring it back tomorrow, I'll..."

The little girl didn't want to hear what he would do. She was already staggering home with the cooking pot in her arms.

The miser hardly

slept that night, worrying about his pot. The next morning he was on his doorstep, watching for his neighbour, and when he saw him coming, he ran forwards eagerly to meet him. As he lifted the pot out of his neighbour's hand, he heard a rattling noise, and looking inside, he saw a little pot nestling inside the big one.

"The most amazing thing has happened," said his neighbour. "During the night your pot gave birth, and I've brought its baby back to you."

The miser was delighted. He'd got something for nothing! He set the little pot on a shelf and rubbed his hands with pleasure.

The next day, the neighbour borrowed the miser's pot again, and again he brought it back with a little one inside.

"It's amazing," he said, "but whenever I borrow something, it gives birth to another."

Gloating, the miser put the second pot next to the first.

"Come again soon!" he called to his departing neighbour. "You can borrow whatever you like!"

Ten days later, a knock on the door came again. There stood the neighbour.

"Please..." he began.

"You want my cooking pot?" cried the miser.

"Take it! But surely one's not enough. Look, here are five. All the pots I've got. Take them! Take them!"

The next day, the miser was up early, licking his lips expectantly.

"Five more little pots today," he thought. "I'll be able to sell them in the market and make a good profit. Now, where's that neighbour of mine? He's usually here by now."

He waited and waited, hopping about impatiently on his doorstep. The sun rose higher and higher in the sky, heating his head under his faded old turban, but still the neighbour didn't come.

At last, the miser could bear it no longer. He ran to his neighbour's house and hammered on the door. His neighbour opened it, and shook his head sadly when he saw the miser.

"Such bad news!" he said. "I was on my way to tell you."

"Bad news? What bad news?" said the miser anxiously.

"Your poor dear cooking pots caught a chill in the night, and they have all passed away. Not one of them was left alive! Such a tragedy!"

The miser stamped his foot.

"What do you mean, my cooking pots passed away? They're only *things*. Things can't die!"

The neighbour smiled.

"You believed that your old pot could give birth to little ones," he said, "so why can't you believe that they've died?"

The miser stared at him speechlessly.

"You've tricked me!" he shouted.

"No," said the neighbour. "I've taught you a lesson. Don't be so mean and greedy in future. Give and lend what you have, and only then will God bless you."

The miser went off, scowling furiously, but he must have learned something, because when he got home, he put a saucer of milk out for his cat.

The Moon Pool

Once upon a time, drought came to the Land of the Elephants. Month after month the sun shone pitilessly down, and the sky, clouded with dust, was the colour of brass. The streams and wells dried to muddy trickles, the grass became brittle and brown, and the leaves hung limply on the skeleton trees.

The elephants, tired of the poor water and meagre food in their country, longed to drink

deeply in cool, clear pools, and eat their fill of lush new grass. They went to their king and told him what they wanted.

The King of the Elephants flapped his dusty ears.

"This is what I long for, too," he told his subjects. "I'll send scouts out into other lands to find water. Then we'll go there and take it, however far we have to travel."

A few days later, his scouts returned.

"We've found a beautiful pool, the coolest and freshest we have ever seen," they told their king. "It's known as the Moon Pool. It lies in a valley between high crags. The grass there is long and lush and sweet, and delicious fruits drip from the trees. There's only one problem: the valley is in the Land of the Hares, and the water and everything that is there belongs to them."

The King of the Elephants waved his trunk dismissively.

"Hares?" he scoffed. "Little weak creatures no bigger than our feet? There's no danger from them. We'll soon kick them out of the way. Now, lead us to this wonderful place. I can't wait to take a trunkful of this pure water and squirt it all over my back."

Off trouped the elephants, trumpeting with excitement, running faster and faster as they entered the green valley and smelled the water of the Moon Pool. They took no notice of the hares, who tried helplessly to bar their way. They trampled them carelessly underfoot, parents and young alike, killing and injuring them in the stampede. When they reached the pool, they waded into it, drinking their fill, wallowing in the water and splashing each other, driving away with lunges of their tusks any timid hare who dared to come near them.

The hares, dismayed and terrified, clustered round their king.

"What can we do?" they wailed. "How can we drive these brutes out of our country?"

The King of the Hares, looking round his frightened subjects, asked for their ideas, but none of them could think of any way to free themselves from their tormentors.

At last, Firuz, a hare of great wisdom and nobility, spoke up.

"O King, May You Live For Ever," she said, "let me go and speak to the King of the Elephants. I'm sure I can find a way to bring our troubles to an end."

The King of the Hares admired and trusted Firuz, who was the mother of many fine sons and daughters.

"Go then, and do your best," he said. "But speak to their king gently. Don't threaten him or show your anger. If you do, he will never listen to you, because he is strong, and all the power is in his hands. You will only make him bully us even more."

Firuz nodded at the words of her king.

"I must be clever if I'm to speak to the Elephant King," she told herself. "If I go too close, one of these giant beasts might crush me under their feet."

Firuz waited until night had fallen and the full moon, a huge ball of shining silver, had risen above the pool. Then she bounded to the top of the nearest crag and called out, in her clear, high voice, "Elephants! Listen to me! Call your king to speak to me!"

The elephants, who had drunk their fill of water and eaten as much grass and fruit as their huge stomachs could hold, were settling down to sleep. They looked round, trying to see where the bell-like voice was coming from.

Firuz lay down at the edge of the crag above

them, and laid her long ears flat against her back so that she was all but invisible from below.

"Elephants!" she called again in her sweetest voice. "Call your king!"

The King of the Elephants, trying to follow the sound of her voice, approached the foot of the cliff. He looked up, but saw only the moon floating serenely overhead.

"Who dares to call me?" he bellowed. "Who are you? What do you want?"

"I am a messenger sent from the Moo-oo-oon," Firuz sang back, her voice echoing from crag to crag across the valley. "She has sent me to tell you what is in her heart."

The King of the Elephants stepped back. No creature on earth was bigger than him. No animal was stronger. Fear had always been unknown to him. But now the moon, in the power of her brilliance, was sending a shiver like a shard of glass through his heart.

"Tell me, then," he said in a gentler voice. "What does the Moon want to say to me?"

"Here is her message," fluted Firuz. "She sends it only for the good of your people. Disaster threatens you, O King. Listen and be warned."

The King of the Elephants took another step backwards, and lowered his trunk.

"Disaster?" he repeated.

"Strong creatures can bully the weak," Firuz went on. "They can go where they like. They can trample and hurt any they choose, as you have done to the hares. You thought that no one could stand in your way. You have even invaded the pool dedicated to my mistress, churned up her banks with your heavy feet and stirred up her water, polluting it with your filth."

No one had ever dared to criticize the King of the Elephants before.

"What can the Moon do to me and my people?" he blustered, raising his head so that the light glittered along the sharp ivory of his long white tusks. "If she thinks she can threaten us, you can tell her that she's wrong. We elephants fear no one, and we never will."

"Be careful, Elephant King," Firuz called back in her most ethereal voice. "Danger is near.

The Moon has the power of sight. If you make her angry, she will blind you. She will destroy your eyes and you will wander the world helplessly for ever more."

Ever more! Ever more! echoed round the valley.

A sharper shaft of fear struck at the Elephant King. He shut his eyes involuntarily and opened them again, breathing out with relief when the moonlit world in all its soft brilliance reappeared around him.

"How do I know that you're telling the truth?" he called out, trying to sound brave again. "How can I be sure that this is not a trick?"

Firuz was ready for this.

"Go to the pool now," she sang back. "Stand at the edge, and the Moon will meet you there."

The Elephant King, trying to hide his fear, strutted to the pool and looked down into its depths. The moon's reflection, round and perfect in the still water, shone back at him.

"It's true then," he told himself. "This is something greater even than me." And his knees trembled.

"Draw water into your trunk," commanded Firuz, "and wash your face. Then kneel. Kneel to the Moon, Elephant King!"

The King of the Elephants drew water into his trunk and sprayed his face, then he fell to his knees. As he did this, the moon's reflection trembled and shattered into a thousand pieces like sharp slivers of crystal, stinging his eyes.

He groaned in terror, and leaped back out of the water.

"Why does the Moon tremble and break into pieces?" he called out, unable to hide the fear in his voice. "Is she angry with me because I went into her pool?"

"Yes! Yes! Yes!" cried out Firuz, her voice sweet no longer, but full of steel. "Bow to her, Elephant King. Confess your fault, before she enters your eyes and destroys them. Promise that you will never again bully the weak, and take from them what is not yours."

Humbly, the King of the Elephants did as he was told. He laid his great body down in the dust and made his subjects do the same. They told the Moon that they were sorry, and would never commit such crimes again.

Before the sun had risen, the elephants had filed out of the Land of the Hares and returned to their own land, to wait patiently until the rains came to fill their own rivers and make their own grass grow green.

As for the hares, they lived in peace and happiness in the valley by the Moon Pool for the rest of their days.

The Suit of Stone

Once there lived a boastful tailor. He spent his days stitching and snipping and selling his wares, and all the time he never stopped bragging about himself.

"See this?" he'd say, strutting about with a piece of silk in his hands. "I'm going to make the best suit in all Baghdad out of this. I'm the only man who can do it, too. Even the robe I made for the Caliph's second cousin's father-in-law, which – credit where it's due – was a miracle of tailoring, wasn't half as good as this one's going to be."

The boastful tailor showed off to everyone who came into his shop, puffing out his chest and nodding at his own cleverness.

"I see you're admiring my new lamp," he'd remark to a yawning customer. "Handsomest thing you ever saw, isn't it? A grateful father gave it to me after I rescued his son from three blood-thirsty bandits who attacked him on the road. I drove them off all by myself, armed with nothing but these sewing scissors."

The tailor even boasted about the canary he kept in a cage by the door.

"Best singer in the city," he told anyone who would listen. "There's not another bird who can reach those top notes and scratch his beak at the same time."

Soon everyone was tired of the boastful tailor. Rumours of him even reached the Caliph.

"That fellow should be taught a lesson," said the Caliph, "before he puffs himself up so much that he bursts. Bring him to the palace garden."

The tailor was delighted to be summoned to the Caliph's palace and hurried off at once.

"Can't stop to talk!" he called out to everyone as he passed. "Just off to measure the Caliph for a new suit of clothes. Only the best will do for him! And I am the best, though I say it myself."

He waved the servants aside and hurried to the palace garden, where the Caliph was walking with his courtiers.

He stood in front of the Caliph and bowed – but not quite low enough.

What kind of suit would Your Splendidness be wanting?" he asked jauntily. "I have the best range of silks, velvets, cottons or linens – in the

finest colours you'll find anywhere. Choose any material you like. Anything at all."

"Anything?" asked the Caliph softly. "You can make clothes out of anything?"

"Oh yes," beamed the tailor. "Just name your choice, Your Magnificency."

The Caliph pointed to a large stone lying nearby.

"Make me a suit out of that," he said.

The tailor laughed.

"Your Sublimity is joking, of course."

The Caliph's eyebrows snapped together in a thunderous frown.

"Joking? You accuse your Caliph of joking? You boasted that you could make me a suit out of anything. I've told you what I wish for. Take that stone away. I shall expect my suit within three days, and if you haven't brought it to me by then, your head will leave your shoulders."

The tailor went pale and clutched at the nearest courtier, who shook him off disdainfully.

"C-Clothes from a s-stone?" he stammered. "It's impossible! I beg you, Your Majesty! I implore you…!"

But he was speaking to thin air. The Caliph had swept off, with his courtiers running after him.

The tailor tottered home, bowed down under the heavy stone.

News of his commission had already spread round the city.

"Nice little job you've got yourself!" people laughed. "Should be easy for you. You're the best, after all!"

When the tailor reached home, he sank down on to his bed and burst into tears.

Now, the tailor had a wife and three daughters. The two older girls were as silly and vain as their father, but the youngest was sensible and modest. They all clustered round him.

"Oh my poor children!" moaned the tailor. "You're going to be orphans. In three days' time I shall lose my head!" And he told them what had happened.

His wife and two older daughters began to weep and wail, but the youngest sat quietly and thought hard.

"Don't worry, Father," she said at last. "Do as I say, and all will be well."

The next morning the tailor returned to the palace with a bag of sand in his hand.

"Well, my good man?" said the Caliph. "And how is my suit of clothes coming along?"

"All cut out and ready to stitch," the tailor said meekly, "but the work's held up for lack of thread. Your Highness didn't give me any. I've brought this bag of sand, and if you would kindly order some thread to be made from it, I'll start sewing without delay."

The Caliph threw back his head and roared with laughter.

"Very good, my dear fellow. Very clever. Now, whose idea was this?"

The tailor was about to say, "Mine, mine! There's no one who can get the better of me!" – but he stopped himself just in time.

"It was my youngest daughter's idea, sir. She's a very clever girl, and she loves her old father, however foolish he may have been."

"Your daughter, you say?" said the Caliph. "I would like to meet this girl."

So the tailor's daughter was called to the palace, and as soon as the Caliph saw her, he fell in love with her. They were married a week later, and the tailor just had time to make a wedding suit for his new son-in-law – which was nearly as fine as the Caliph's third best coat.

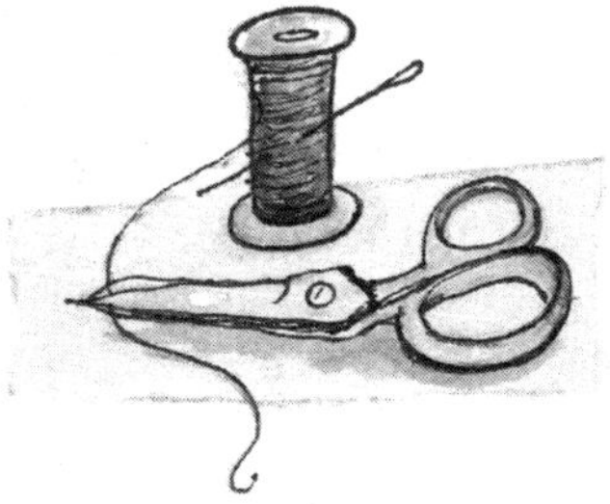

A Fistful of Pearls

Once upon a time there was a merchant who had three daughters. He loved his home and family, but sometimes he had to travel to distant lands, taking goods to sell and buying more to bring home.

One day, before he went away, he said to his daughters, "Now, my dears, what would you like your old father to bring you back? Trinkets? Baubles? Dresses – that sort of thing?"

The oldest girl, who thought a lot about her looks, said, "A dress, Baba! Green, with gold embroidery. I always look best in green."

The second, who was rather silly, said, "A mirror for me, set in gold. My best friend's mirror is only framed in silver."

The youngest daughter, who loved her father dearly, was about to say, "I want nothing, Baba dear, except your safe return," when her mother nudged her and said softly in her ear, "Ask for a fistful of pearls."

The youngest girl was about to object, but her mother pushed her forward, so she said, "A fistful of pearls, please, Baba, if it's not too much trouble."

The next morning, the merchant went down to the sea and stepped aboard his loaded ship, and his daughters watched him from behind their lattice window and waved until the ship was out of sight.

When the merchant reached the far-off city, his business was soon done. He tucked the money he had made into his pocket and went off to the bazaar to buy presents for his daughters. The green dress with gold embroidery was easily found, and so was the mirror in its golden frame. But when he visited the jeweller's shop and asked for a fistful of pearls, the man laughed and said, "A fistful of pearls? You'll have to go to the palace for that."

"The palace?" asked the bewildered merchant.

"Didn't you know?" the jeweller said. "The palace of the Sultan of the Jinns is near here.

Go and ask at his gate for a fistful of pearls – and see what answer you get."

Puzzled, the merchant hurried away with the jeweller's mocking laughter ringing in his ears.

"A strange city this is," he said to himself, "where a jeweller refuses to sell pearls to an honest man. I'll have to try the palace, I suppose. I can't let my dear daughter down."

At the palace of the Sultan, the guards courteously waved the merchant through to an inner courtyard paved in silver and set with rubies and sapphires, where a young man was feeding a pair of doves.

"Excuse me, sir," the merchant said nervously, "but I've come to buy a fistful of pearls."

The young man smiled.

"And why do you want a fistful of pearls?" he asked.

"They're for my daughter," the merchant answered, and he told the young man of his youngest daughter's request.

"Tell me about this daughter of yours," the young man said. "What kind of girl is she?"

The merchant launched at once into a description of his daughter, comparing her beauty to a young gazelle's, her courage to a lion's, and her intelligence to the cleverest of sages.

When he had finished, the young man said, "Your daughter's request was a wise one, sir, for I am Fistful of Pearls. That is my name. I am the son of the Sultan of the Jinns, and I would very much like to meet your daughter."

The merchant, dazzled by the splendour of the palace and the noble bearing of the prince, could only murmur, "Well, yes indeed – honoured, of course, most kind and obliging."

The prince summoned a servant and sent him off to fetch a tiny box, which he placed in the merchant's hands.

"In this box there are three hairs," he told him. "Build your daughter a special room beside your house and let her sit there alone. You tell me that she is brave. Let her prove it. Tell her to rub the hairs together. Whatever happens next, whatever she sees, she mustn't cry out in fear and wonder, or say anything except, "God's will be done!" three times. Then, and only then, will all be well."

The merchant took the box, trying to conceal

a shudder of fear, and hurried away.

"Jinns!" he thought. "There's dangerous magic here. I'll say nothing about all this to my daughter. She must do without her pearls. I'll buy her a pretty ball to make up for it."

When he reached home, his older daughters were delighted with their presents. The first one paraded in her green dress, showing off its lustrous sheen. The second grabbed her mirror and ran to show it to her best friend.

"I'm sorry, my dear," the merchant said to his youngest daughter. "I couldn't remember what you had asked for, so I've brought you this pretty ball."

The girl took the ball, thanked her father and put it away in her chest. She had grown out of playing with a ball years ago, but didn't like to tell him.

The merchant's wife was not put off so easily.

"Well?" she demanded, as soon as she was alone with her husband. "And what about the fistful of pearls?"

The merchant shut the door and lowered his voice, afraid that his daughters might hear.

"My dear," he said earnestly. "You have no idea what you're talking about. Fistful of Pearls is the name of the Prince of the Jinns! What do you think of that? I found myself talking to him, and most alarming it was too. Magic! Sorcery! Enchantment! you know, and all that sort of thing."

His wife didn't seem in the least surprised.

"This prince," she said. "What kind of a man is he? Handsome? Ugly? Old? Young?"

"I have to confess," the merchant said unwillingly, "that Fistful of Pearls is the handsomest young man I have ever seen in my life, and his face shows only goodness and kindness. As for the palace, you can't begin to imagine its magnificence. Even the cage for the prince's doves is made of solid gold. It must be worth a fortune!"

"And did you tell him about our daughter?" asked his wife.

"As a matter of fact, my dear, I did," the merchant said, even less willingly.

"And? What did he say?" urged his wife.

"He said he wished to meet her, and he told me how to summon him. But of course, the whole thing's out of the question! A jinn! For our child! No, no, I'd never permit it."

"But a prince!" said his wife. "And a handsome one too! Think of it, husband. You said yourself he looks kind and good. What harm could he do her, after all?"

From that moment on, the merchant's wife gave him no peace. From morning to night she nagged him about the Prince of the Jinns and what he might do for their daughter, until at last the merchant could resist her no longer.

With the greatest reluctance he built a room at the side of his house and, on his wife's instructions, furnished it with silken hangings. Then his wife dressed the youngest daughter in her prettiest clothes, pressed the box into her hands, told her what to say and do, and left her alone in the room.

Her heart beating fast with fear, the girl shut her eyes tight, opened them wide again, took a deep breath and lifted the lid of the little box. Then she picked up the three hairs that lay inside and rubbed them together.

At once, a wall of the room fell away, and she gasped as a lake of shimmering water appeared. A second later she gasped again, as over the water came sailing a ship made of clear, sparkling crystal. Standing in the prow stood the Prince of the Jinns, the handsomest man she had ever seen.

She was just about to shout, "God save me!" when she remembered her instructions. "God's will be done!" she cried out three times, and then stared in wonder as the prince stepped off

the crystal ship and into her little room.

From then on, the prince and the youngest daughter met every day. They had so much to say to each other that there were never enough hours in the day and the time sped by on wings. The girl lived in a blaze of happiness, and love made her more beautiful than ever.

Her oldest sister grew jealous.

"If it goes on like this, she'll be prettier even than me," she thought. "There's a secret in that room, and I'm going to find out what it is."

She waited until the next day, when her little sister went to the bathhouse. Then she stole the key from her sister's pocket, crept up to the door of the mysterious room, turned the key in the lock and went in.

"But it's just a room," she cried, disappointed. "There's nothing special here at all!"

Her eyes fell on the little box lying on a table. She picked it up and opened it. Inside lay the three little hairs. She picked them up, and as she did so, she rubbed them together. Instantly the wall of the room melted away and the crystal ship, with the Prince of the Jinns standing in the prow, sailed towards her across the shimmering waters of the lake.

Terrified, the oldest sister cried out, "What's this? Who are you? God save me!"

Before she had finished, the crystal ship shattered into a million pieces. Splinters of glass pierced the prince and he gave a terrible cry. The lake faded and disappeared. There was nothing but a solid wall.

"What have I done?" the oldest sister whispered. "Oh, I wish I'd never come in here!"

Quietly she crept out of the room, shut the door behind her, and replaced the key in her sister's pocket.

"I'll say nothing," she told herself. "Perhaps no harm is done."

Her little sister came home from the bathhouse and ran to her room, eager to summon the prince. She wanted to tell him about the kitten she'd seen at the bathhouse, and the roses blooming in her pot, and the riddle she'd learned from her friend. She opened the little box, rubbed the hairs together and waited, a happy smile on her face.

The wall stayed in its place. No lake appeared, no crystal ship with the prince standing in the prow.

The youngest daughter turned pale, and rubbed the hairs together again. But nothing happened.

Again and again she tried, but still her prince didn't come.

Day after day she crept to her room and tried to summon the prince, but he never came. She grew pale and thin. She could neither eat nor sleep. Doctors were called, but none of them could cure her.

At last, her oldest sister, anxious and ashamed, confessed what she had done.

Her little sister had been lying on her bed, her cheeks wet with tears, but now she sat up, wiped her eyes, and said, "If he's wounded, he can't come to me, so I shall go to him."

Her mother and sisters shook their heads.

"The poor child is raving," they told each other. "How can she travel anywhere, young and sick as she is?"

But that night, the little sister slipped out of her father's house and set off to find her prince. She travelled by day and night, over mountains and deserts, across rivers and seas, asking everywhere for the palace of the Jinns.

No one could help her. No one had heard of it.

At last, one weary evening, she sank down under a tree to rest. But as she closed her eyes, she heard the cooing of doves in the branches above. To her amazement, she understood their words.

One said:

Coo, sister, coo!
Where are you?
If this girl is asleep, there's no more to be done,
But if she's awake, the prize will be won!

At once, such a cooing and a fluting broke out that the little sister had a hard time making head or tail of it, but at last she understood that they were giving her instructions.

She held out her hands. Two white doves fluttered down to perch on them. Carefully she pulled a feather from each of them and plucked a handful of leaves from the tree; then, in desperate haste, she ran in the direction they had shown her.

A little while later, she came to the palace of the Sultan of Jinns.

The gatekeeper shook his head sorrowfully when she asked to see the prince.

"The poor young man is at death's door,"

he said. "No one is allowed to see him."

"But I can cure him! Let me in!" the little sister cried, and pushed past him into the palace.

She ran down the gold and silver corridors, never noticing the splendour of it all, until at last she came to the place where the prince was lying, his father and mother sitting anxiously by his side. His face was still and bloodless, and his hands lay limply by his side.

"Too late!" she thought. "I've come too late!"

But she ran up and touched him, first with one feather, then with the other.

At once, the splinters of crystal that had pierced the prince's body fell out. Then she wiped his wounds with the leaves she had brought, and they were instantly healed. Colour returned to the prince's face. He opened his eyes and saw the little sister.

"Who are you?" he said. "How did you heal me?"

"Don't you know me?" she answered. "You used to come to me in your crystal ship. When I heard what my sister had done, I came in search of you."

Then the prince recognised her, and was filled with joy.

They were married at once, in a wedding that lasted for three whole days. And they lived happily together for the rest of their lives in the country of the Jinns.

The Sign of the Tassel

Once there was a shopkeeper who had a very bad temper. When he was happy, he was the kindest man in all Iraq, but when he was angry he stamped about the house, he smashed the dishes in the kitchen, and he scared his wife so much that she hid herself in a cupboard.

One morning, after a night when her husband had been raging and storming, she said to him, "My dear, you have a very bad temper."

"Oh I know, I know," he said apologetically. "I can't help myself. When things go wrong in the shop, and my customers insult me, and my assistant cheats me, and the rain comes in and makes all my cloth go mouldy, it puts me in such a rage that I just have to let it all out when I come home."

"I quite understand," she said, "but the problem is that I have a very bad temper too."

"You?" he said, astonished. "But you're always so sweet and kind."

She scowled and tried to look furious.

"You've never seen me when I get angry! Once, when my brother called me names, I picked up a stick and beat him till he screamed for mercy, and he was much bigger than me."

"Surely not," her husband said, backing away from her.

"And once, when my big sister laughed at me, I scratched her face and pulled her hair till it came out in clumps."

"Oh," said her husband thoughtfully.

"And you know what really worries me?" his wife went on – "what might happen if we both got into a bad temper at the same time. We might hurt each other!"

"That would be terrible," murmured her husband, sidling towards the door.

"Don't go away!" she said. She stopped scowling and smiled at him. "I've thought of a way round this problem. What we need to do is warn each other when we're feeling angry. We must agree on a sign. If I see your sign, I'll know you're in a temper and I'll try to control mine, and you must do the same for me."

"What sort of a sign?" asked her husband.

"*I* don't know," she answered, looking fierce again. "Can't you think of something?"

Her husband thought hard.

"I know," he said at last. "When I'm in a rage, I'll turn the tassel round on my fez when I'm walking home so that it hangs down over my face."

"What a good idea!" nodded his wife. "And I'll put on my white apron, so that when you walk in through the door you'll see I'm in a temper and you'll make allowances for me."

From that day on, the shopkeeper's wife watched every day at the window when her husband was due to come home. If she saw him marching up the street with a face like thunder and the tassel of his fez swishing backwards and forwards across his nose like the tail of an angry cat, she rushed to put on her white apron. When her husband saw it, he pushed the tassel of his fez to the

side, pushing his temper away at the same time.

When this had happened several times, he said to his wife, "My love, isn't it odd that our fits of temper always occur at the same time? Why do you think that is?"

"It's the strangest thing!" she agreed. "But have you noticed that we've both managed to control our tempers all this time? You never smash my dishes any more, no matter how angry you feel, and I haven't torn any of your clothes to shreds."

"You're right," he said. "Now we know how to do it, I don't think we need bother with our signs any more."

And the shopkeeper and his wife lived together in perfect harmony for the rest of their lives.

A Coat for a King

Once there was a wolf. He ran about the hills all day long catching lambs that strayed from the shepherd's flock and crunching them up, bones and all, for his dinner.

But one day, as the wolf circled hungrily round the sheep trying to decide which lamb to leap on, he stumbled and fell, tumbling down the mountainside, ears over tail, towards a well in the valley below. The next thing he knew, he was plunging down into a deep dark hole, to land with a splash in the water.

He pulled himself up on to a ledge and squatted just above the surface of the water.

"This ain't no joke," he told himself. "A right pickle I've got myself into. What have you gone and done, Wolfie? How are you goin' to get yourself out of this?"

He scratched his ears, licked his paws, and thought long and hard. Then a smile curved his long hungry jaws, and he nodded to himself, gave a mighty yawn and settled down for a nap.

He woke with a start to see a large face surrounded by a tawny mane peering down at him from the rim of the well above.

"Here comes the lion for his evening drink," thought the wolf. "Now then, my old son, here's your chance."

He began to sing a cheerful little song:

"Sew and stitch,
Stitch and sew,
Nip and tuck
And here we go!"

"I say," the lion called out in his deep, majestic voice. "Is someone down there?"

"*Sew and stitch, stitch and sew...*" the wolf went on, pretending not to hear.

"What's going on down there?" said the lion. "Has somebody fallen down the well? Is everything all right?"

"Eh? Did someone call?" said the wolf, sounding surprised. "Oh, it's you, Your Majesty.

Sorry, I'm sure. When I start work, I'm so busy I don't hear nothing. Anything I can do for you this fine evenin'?"

"Do for me?" said the lion, raising his mighty brows until they almost met his mane. "Whatever could a fellow do for a chap when he's lurking down a well?"

"Do? Do?" said the wolf. "Why, surely Your Majesty knows me? I'm the wolf who makes sheepskin coats. Finest garments in the country. My coats, they keep everyone cosy on long winter nights. All snuggly and warm my customers are, like baby bunnies in a burrow. Now, no disrespect, but I must get back to work. Got to keep the customers happy. List of orders as long as my arm. *Sew and stitch, stitch and sew...*"

"Sorry to butt in, and all that," said the lion, "but I rather fancy one of your coats myself. Snug as a baby bunny, you say? The nights really are frightfully cold these days out on the mountainside. Put me down for one, would you?"

"Oh now," said the wolf, pretending to think. "That could be a problem, Your Maj, what with the demand. But I like to oblige, especially royalty. I tell you what, I'll put you up to the top of the list. Get started on a coat for you tomorrow, I will."

"My dear fellow! How splendid!" said the lion, drawing up the bucket to take a drink.

"But there is the little question of supply," said the wolf. "The raw materials for the job. Think about it, my lord. A bloke can't make a sheepskin coat without the skins of sheep, can he? A good coat, now, it takes a load of sheepskins."

"*Haw, haw!*" laughed the lion. "You can leave that side of things to me. I've been catching sheep since before my whiskers grew."

"Right then, sir. You got yourself a deal," smirked the wolf. "You supply the sheep, I supply the coat. Simple as that."

"Absolutely," agreed the lion. "You shall have your sheep tomorrow."

The wolf snoozed on his ledge all that night, and the next morning, just as the sun rose in an orb of gold over the horizon, two fat lambs splashed down into the well beside him.

"There you are," said the lion. "I'll be back for my coat this evening."

"Oh sir!" objected the wolf, sounding shocked. "A couple of lambs, fine as these ones undoubtedly are, wouldn't make a coat for the runt of a wolf's litter, never mind one for a magnificent personage such as your Royal Self."

The lion stroked his whiskers with one elegant paw.

"I take your point. More shall be forthcoming," he said, and off he strolled to begin his hunt.

As soon as he had gone, the wolf fell upon the lambs and gobbled them up – wool, bones, hooves and all.

The next day, the lion came back with another lamb, and two the day after that, and three on the third day, and four on the fourth, and the wolf ate all of them, down to the last woolly tail.

At the end of a week, the wolf was growing fat and the lion was growing impatient.

"Look here, old boy, where's my coat?" he growled down the well shaft. "You've had a whole flock of sheep. Surely that's enough for a chestful of coats."

"Now, Your Majesty," chided the wolf. "We're talking about a quality product here, not just any old thing! A couple more days, a few more lambs, and you'll have a right royal robe what'll

make you the envy of all your subjects for miles around. But good workmanship don't come quick. Only the best will do for a monarch, after all."

"Oh very well," said the lion. "But do hurry up, there's a good chap. The winter's coming on and I'm feeling the cold. Last night my mane was frozen stiff."

Another few days passed, more lambs met their end in the wolf's jaws, and now the wolf was so fat he had almost outgrown his ledge.

The lion, meanwhile, was losing his temper.

"I've had enough of this!" he roared down the well one morning, and in his voice was the unmistakable rumble of majesty. "If my coat's not ready by tomorrow, you'll pay dearly for your impudence."

The wolf shivered.

"He is a lion, and a king, after all," he told himself. "Oh well, all good things come to an end. And anyway, this ledge is too small, and it's really boring being stuck down here all day long."

"No need to get upset, sir," he called up to the lion. "Your coat's ready at last. Beautiful piece of work, though I say it myself. Now, if you'll kindly throw down a rope, I'll tie the coat to it and you can pull it up."

"About time too," the lion said, picking up the rope that lay near the top of the well and throwing one end of it down to the wolf.

The wolf picked up two mangy old sheepskins that he had kept for this emergency, and caught hold of the rope.

"Haul away, Your Majesty!" he called out. "Here it comes! A coat of quality! A coat to die for! A coat fit for a king!"

The lion began to pull the wolf up, but the wolf was now so fat and heavy that the lion's muscles were straining, and he was panting with the effort.

"Good heavens!" he puffed. "What a weight! I never knew – *ee* – that a coat – *ah* – could be so heavy."

"Oh, it's the dampness sir. The moisture's caught in the wool. The minute it dries out, it'll be as light as thistledown. You'll see."

A few minutes later, the wolf was at the top of the well. The lion fell over, exhausted and breathless on the ground.

"Here's your coat, Your Majesty!" shouted the wolf, flinging the two sheepskins at the lion. Then, before the lion could stagger to his feet, he was off and away running for his life into the far mountains.

As for the lion, he slunk off to nurse his wounded pride under a spreading fig tree.

"How ever could I have let myself be tricked by such a scoundrel?" he asked himself, shaking his mane furiously. Then he lifted his head and roared, and the angry echo pursued the wolf into the rocky heights, and made all the sheep in the valley shiver in their woolly coats.

I Want my Son!

Once there was a widow who lived all alone with her daughter.

One night, someone knocked on their door. The old woman ran to open it and there, on the step, stood a handsome stranger.

"Excuse me for disturbing you," he said, "but I've lost my way, and it's late, and I'm tired, and……"

"Say no more!" the widow said kindly. "Come in and make yourself at home."

Gratefully the stranger stepped inside. The old woman took him upstairs to her sitting room and he sank down on the cushions she brought out for him, glad to rest his weary legs.

The old woman hurried back to the kitchen where her daughter was waiting.

"Quick," she said. "Put water on to boil. We must cook a good dinner for our guest."

"What guest? Who is it?" asked her daughter.

"He's a stranger who's lost his way," answered her mother. "He's very handsome, and he speaks nicely and looks kind. He's just the sort of man I'd like you to marry."

The daughter, full of curiosity, stole up the stairs and peeped in through the door of the sitting room, then tiptoed back to the kitchen.

"Oh, Mother!" she said. "If only I could find a husband like that!"

"What a wedding it would be," her mother sighed. "I'm sure he'd give you a beautiful dowry, and I'd buy you the finest wedding clothes, and we'd make a marvellous feast. Think of the roasted lambs and buttered chickens, and rice studded with almonds, and stuffed vegetables, and delicious sherbets!"

"And all the guests would come in their best clothes," her daughter chimed in, "and they'd give us lovely presents – silver mirrors, and inlaid trays, and silks from Damascus."

"And a year would go by and you'd have a beautiful baby boy," her mother said, her eyes shining at the thought. "Just think how sweet he'd be!"

"He'd have a chubby little face, and strong little legs, and he'd learn to walk in next to no time," said her daughter dreamily.

"Yes, and he'd climb up the stairs all the way

to the roof, and shout down, 'Look at me, Granny! I'm a big boy now!'"

The girl clapped her hand over her mouth in horror.

"But there's no railing round the roof! He'll fall down on to the hard stones and die!"

"Oh, what a tragedy! Oh, how terrible!" cried her mother. Her eyes filled with tears, and so did her daughter's. They both began to cry noisily.

The stranger, sitting in the room above, had heard every word. He ran down the stairs calling out, "What have you done with my son? How could you be so careless! I want my son!"

Mother and daughter looked at each other and burst out laughing. The mother ran out of the kitchen, scarlet with embarrassment.

"Oh sir, please forgive us," she said. "We were just being silly."

The stranger smiled at her.

"It didn't sound silly to me. It sounded wonderful. And your daughter has the sweetest voice I've ever heard. I'm sure her beauty matches it."

"Oh it does, it does!" the old woman said, running into the kitchen and bringing out her blushing daughter.

The girl and the stranger fell in love at once, and the wedding was celebrated a month later. The bridegroom gave his bride a handsome dowry.

Her mother bought her the best wedding clothes, and at the wedding feast there were roasted lambs and buttered chickens, and rice studded with almonds, and stuffed vegetables, and delicious sherbets.

The guests came in their best clothes, and they gave the happy couple lovely presents – silver mirrors, and inlaid trays, and silks from Damascus.

A year to the day after the wedding, the bride gave birth to a beautiful baby boy, but before he learned to walk, his granny built a good strong railing round the roof of the house.

And they all praised Allah, who had given them their hearts' desire.

Acknowledgements

With grateful thanks to the authors of the following books, from which these stories have been adapted:

Tales from the Arab Tribes, C.G.Campbell (Lindsay Drummond, 1949).

Folktales from the City of the Golden Domes, Sarah Powell Jamali (Khayats, 1965).

Folktales of Iraq, E.S. Stevens (Oxford University Press, 1931).

Arab Folktales, Inea Bushnaq (Penguin, 1986)

The Fables of Kalilah and Dimnah, Saleh Sa'adeh Jallad (transl.) (Melisende, 2002.)

Note: The Fables of Kalilah and Dimnah originated in Kashmir and were first written down in Sanskrit, but they were translated into Arabic in the eighth century and have been a much-loved part of Iraqi folklore ever since.

Elizabeth Laird lived for six months in Iraq, where her husband worked with the British Council, then moved to Beirut during the civil war and was evacuated to Vienna. Travel has always been an important part of her writing, and she frequently visits Ethiopia, her favourite place in the world, collecting stories from indigenous storytellers. She is constantly surprised by the common themes and characters running through stories from different parts of the world, while at the same time relishing the differences in individual cultural traditions. Among her many children's novels – which have won her four shortlistings for the Carnegie Medal – are *Red Sky in the Morning, Kiss the Dust* and *Secret Friends*. Elizabeth divides her time between London and Edinburgh.

Ghaddar the Ghoul
and other Palestinian Stories

Sonia Nimr
Illustrated by Hannah Shaw
Introduced by Ghada Karmi

Why do Snakes eat Frogs?
What makes a Ghoul turn Vegetarian?
How can a Woman make a Bored Prince Smile?

The answers to these and many other questions can be found in this delicious anthology of Palestinian folk stories. A wry sense of humour runs through their cast of characterful women, genial tricksters and mischievous animals. Sonia Nimr's upbeat storytelling, bubbling with wit and humour, will delight readers discovering for the first time the rich tradition of Palestinian storytelling.

ISBN: 978-1-84507-523-1

The Prince Who Thought he was a Rooster and other Jewish Stories

Ann Jungman
Illustrated by Sarah Adams

A Chilli Champion?… a Golem?…
a Prince who thinks he's a Rooster?

Find them all in this collection of traditional Jewish tales – lovingly treasured, retold and carried through countries as far apart as Poland, Tunisia, Czechoslovakia, Morocco, Russia and Germany, with a cast of eccentric princes, flustered tailors, wise rabbis and the oldest champion of all! Seasoned with wit, humour and magic, Ann Jungman's retellings of stories familiar to Jewish readers are sure to delight a new, wider readership.

ISBN: 978-1-84507-794-5

The Dragon of Krakow
and other Polish Stories

Richard Monte
Illustrated by Paul Hess

These Polish folk tales have a delightfully mischievous character all their own. To create his sparkling collection, Richard Monte has gathered some of Poland's favourite stories from all over the country: *The Golden Duck* hails from Warsaw, *The King Who Was Eaten by Mice* comes from Gniezno, *The Gingerbread Bees* is from Torun, while *The Dragon of Krakow* tells the legendary story of King Krak and how his beautiful city came to be built. Brimming with humour, magic and Paul Hess's exuberant illustrations, the retellings uncover a fascinating land and people.

ISBN 978-1-84507-752-5